Hello Mr Elephant?

I dedicate this book to
My two darling Granddaughters
whom I love with all my heart

I sat on a bench and looked over the sea
and what did I see looking back at me?

An elephant I exclaimed that cannot be
elephants don't swim I'm sure you'll agree

Hello Mr elephant are you ok?
You shouldn't be playing in the bay

Fish live in there and big sharks too
They will be happy to make a meal out of you

Hello Mr elephant don't go away
I'm ready to rescue you from the bay

Hello Mr elephant I can't see you anymore
I hope you didn't sink to the ocean floor

Hello Mr elephant where did you go
Oh, there you are bobbing to and fro

Hello Mr elephant I'm with you now
Get into the boat & sit at the bow

Your image has changed now I don't understand
As you stand in front of me on the sand

Your ears are gone and your nose is small
And to be quite honest you're not very tall

You're not an elephant it's plain to see
You look more like a shark oh deary me
With your big white teeth grinning back at me

Sorry Mr shark please don't eat me
I thought you were an elephant drowning in the sea

I will take you back home don't you worry
Its only a short trip and I will do it in a hurry

Hello Mr Shark you're back to where you started
I think it's time that you and I were parted

Hello Little boy where do you think you're going
I hope you don't think you're going to do a bit of rowing

You see I'm a little hungry and it's time for my tea
so you young man are going to come with me

Hello Mr Shark what are you going to make
I'm hungry too and wouldn't mind a piece of hake

Hello little boy, it's you I want to eat
Your look very tasty and full of lovely meat

Hello little boy, I want you to know
I am not going to eat you so you are free to go

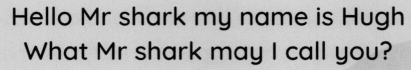

Hello Mr shark my name is Hugh
What Mr shark may I call you?

Call me a cab you silly little boy
I'm not real I'm only a toy!

And the water you're sitting in is warm and soapy
It's a bath you fool, don't be so dopey!

Printed in Great Britain
by Amazon

30959099R00016

Little Hugh sat on a bench and found himself
thrown into a wonderful water world filled
with imagination and rhyme

Author: Jayne Mac

ISBN:9798415092413

ISBN 9798415092413

9000

9 798415 092413

The Nativity Story

The First Christmas for Kids

A long time ago, God sent one of his angels, Gabriel, to the town of Nazareth in Judea (modern-day Israel). God sent Gabriel from heaven to give a message to a young woman named Mary. Mary was engaged to be married to a man named Joseph.

Luke 1:26

The angel told Mary, "Rejoice, you highly favored one!
The Lord is with you. Blessed are you among women!"

At first Mary was confused and did not know
what the angel meant by this.

The angel told Mary not to be afraid and
that God was pleased with her. He said, "You will become
pregnant by the Holy Spirit and have a baby named Jesus."

Gabriel told Mary that Jesus would be the Son of God
and would rule over a kingdom that would never end.

Mary agreed to carry out God's plan.

Luke 1:28-38

Mary went to visit her cousin Elizabeth and her husband Zacariah. Elizabeth knew that Mary had been chosen to be the mother of Jesus and she said to her: "Blessed are you among women, and blessed is the fruit of your womb!"

Mary stayed with Elizabeth and Zacariah for three months and then she returned home.

Luke 1:39-56

An angel also visited Joseph in a dream. He told Joseph that Mary would have a son and that they should name him Jesus. He said that Jesus would be a savior who would save people from sin.

Matthew 2:18-24

At this time, the land of Judea where Mary and Joseph lived was part of the Roman Empire. The ruler of the empire was named Caesar Augustus.

Caesar wanted all of the people in the empire to be counted in a census so they could pay taxes. He said that everyone had to return to the place they were born so they could be counted.

People all across the land traveled back to their home towns.

Luke 2:1-3

Mary and Joseph traveled from Nazareth to Bethlehem, the town where Joseph's family was from.

Luke 2:4

It was a long journey, about 70 miles. Since Mary was pregnant with baby Jesus, she rode on a donkey.

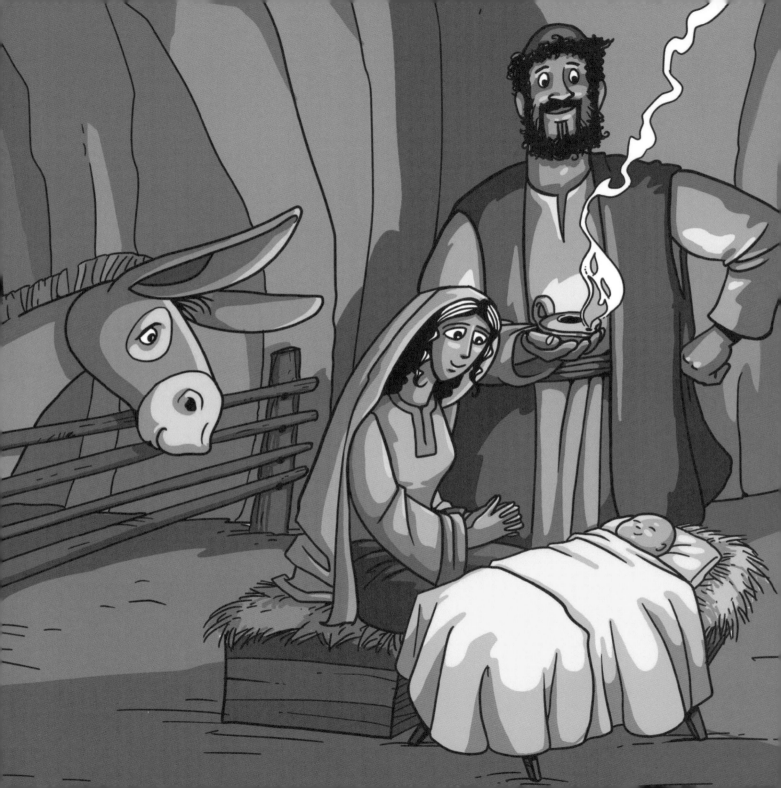

The only place that they could find to stay
was in the barn
where the animals slept.

That night, Mary gave birth to baby Jesus.

Mary and Joseph wrapped their baby boy in a
blanket and placed him in the manger to sleep.

Luke 2:6-7

There were shepherds nearby watching over their sheep.

Luke 2:8

An angel from heaven appeared before the shepherds. He was surrounded by the glory of God and they were afraid.

Luke 2:9

The angel told them not to be afraid because he had good news:
"Today a savior is born in Bethlehem who is Christ the Lord."

Luke 1:26

The angel told the shepherds they would find
baby Jesus lying in the manger.

Luke 2:12

Then many more angels appeared in the sky.

Luke 2:13

The angels began to sing: "Glory to God in the highest, on earth peace, good will toward men."

Luke 2:14

After the angels left the shepherds decided to go to Bethlehem to see if they could find baby Jesus.

When Jesus was born a new star appeared in the sky.
Wise men from the east saw this star.

They followed the star because they knew
it meant that a new king had been born.

Matthew 2:1-2

The wise men followed the star and found Jesus in Bethlehem and brought him gifts. They brought gifts of gold, frankincense, and myrrh.

Matthew 2:11

King Herod, who was the ruler of Judea, found out about a new king being born and he was angry. He was afraid that the new king would take his place.

Matthew 2:3

King Herod ordered his men to find Jesus and get rid of him.

Matthew 2:16

An angel warned Joseph in a dream that they were in danger. Joseph and Mary took baby Jesus and escaped to Egypt where they were safe from King Herod.

Matthew 2:13-14

That is the story of the birth of Jesus and now we celebrate
his birthday every year on Christmas.